# Professor Potts

# Pedals the Canoe

## Steve Boorman

Published by New Generation Publishing in 2020

First Edition

Paperback: 978-1-80031-964-6
Hardback: 978-1-80031-965-3
Ebook: 978-1-80031-966-0

**www.newgeneration-publishing.com**

New Generation Publishing

Professor Potts and his pet parrot Einstein love to invent things. They especially like bicycles.

On Wednesday they were making a shopping bicycle. Sparks were flying everywhere.

Even into a box of paper.

'Oh boswangle', said the professor, as Einstein put out the fire with his cup of tea.

'Hello Dami,' said Professor Potts. 'I'm just making a special shopping bicycle'.

'I've been given a canoe,' said Dami, 'but I can't get it to the river. Can you help me?'

'We need a new bicycle for that,' said the professor. 'I think I can change this one.'

'It's going to be wibbly wobbly,' said Einstein.

'It will be fine,' replied Professor Potts.

'Let's try it,' said Professor Potts.

'Whoah! This is tricky!' he shouts.

'Oh, **winklebirtle**,' could be heard from inside the bush.

The car and trailer had given the professor an idea.

Professor Potts says, 'This should work,' as he tries to peddle.

The canoe **was** too heavy for the professor.

'Oh, nocklesnout,' he said 'I wasn't strong enough to pedal on my own.' Then he had another idea.

'A **two-person** bicycle, that's **what we need.**'

'It's too long,' says Einstein. 'It will be fine,' laughed Professor Potts.

'I knew this would work,' the professor chuckled. 'Sharp bend ahead,' warned Einstein.

'Phew! That was a bit close,' said the professor.

'Oh, anklewiggle,' said Professor Potts.

Then he remembered the motorbike. 'I've got an even better idea,' he said.

'It's definitely going to work this time, Dami,' the professor said.

'I knew it would work.
Now for the bridge.'

'Too Fast!' squawked a very nervous Einstein.

'I'm looking forward to this,' said Dami. 'Me too' said the professor, fighting with his life jacket.

'Oops, sorry Einstein!' laughed the professor.